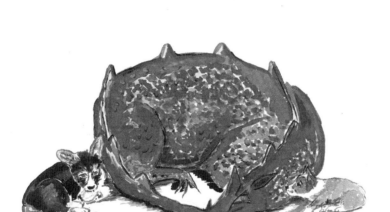

The Secret of the Dragon

For the Wilhelms
Will, Edwin, and Lillian
Lauren and Sophie
Miles

with special thanks to Ch Nodrog Honey

THE SECRET of the DRAGON

Jan E Irving

erinrac.com

Erinrac Enterprises

published by
Erinrac Enterprises
PO Box 313
Upper Beaconsfield
Victoria 3808
Australia

phone 03 59443383
email office@erinrac.com
http://www.erinrac.com

typeset by Erinrac Enterprises

Back cover photo by RMH Irving

Introduction

Welcome to my first fictional story and naturally my first children's story. As I grew up with dogs and have always adored fairy and dragon stories it shouldn't really be surprising that I have actually written *The Secret of the Dragon*. It comes after several reference books on Clumber Spaniels and numerous management articles for all dog breeds, and of course the one-time standard reference for Cashmere Goats.

No doubt, the senior readers will be curious to know what inspired *The Secret of the Dragon*, I can only suggest a lapse of many years since I last read a fairy tale and the keen study and observation of many, many breeds while I was writing *The White Spaniel* which covers the evolution and development of the Clumber. Pembrokes have always surrounded my life as my mother has owned them since 1946 and I readily admit that Ed Presnall's incredible flair for writing a tale at least inspired me to have a go even if I haven't managed to capture his panache at writing. There has also, of course, been the arrival of several nieces and nephews and friends' children that should have tweaked the idea many moons ago.

No, *The Secret of the Dragon* is not the only idea I have; already nearing production are stories on the evolution of the Irish Water Spaniel and Shetland Sheepdog. Trapped within the mists of my mind is the ground for one such tale about Clumbers too; although it is much more elusive! The actual telling of this story hasn't been the hold up in reaching publication. The delay has been due to a need to dust off my painting skills and find a suitable publishing format.

Jan Irving

2

I have a story to tell you. A story handed down from generation to generation since the time when people first arrived on the hillsides of Wales. From the time of magicians, enchantresses, and dragons. From a time before everyone spoke a single tongue and a time when only potions and spells were written down.

It is a story that has passed from the second daughter of a wise and learned man from this long ago period, to her second daughter. The story has passed from second daughter to second daughter for twenty two generations and only now do I know the story of Dragons and Pembrokes and Cardigans. For two thousand years this tale has been guarded and passed from second daughter to second daughter. Now the line of descent has ended. The last of this line, an enchantress herself, has passed the secret to me with the charter to tell all about the dragons of Wales. Only now her line of transmission has ended will this story be told - but this was foretold by the father of the first of the second daughters.

This is a tale more precious than the diamonds of South Africa, with more warmth than the coal of the Welsh hills themselves. It is the tale of the taming of the Welsh dragon and the legacy of that magic.

When humans first came to Wales they travelled with small horses, sheep, cattle, goats, poultry and dogs. They found a wondrous land of enormous hills swathed in the lushest deep green grass, the ridges topped with rocky crusts and short fragrant heath. A land of immeasurably deep and dark valleys. A place of fierce and strong winds and eerie mists.

The first settlers moved through the hills and camped. As they found the nicest places to live, they built small low houses. Local rock was collected to build bridges, roads and houses. In the evenings wisps of light, sweet smelling smoke from the heath fires in the cottages meandered into the air. The horses foaled, the sheep lambed, the cattle calved, chicks hatched, dogs whelped, and human children came for several years. Times were pleasant and idyllic, food was plentiful, rock easily gathered for building, heath was abundant for the fires. But as the population grew, so the resources dwindled and small fights broke out amongst neighbours first, then the stock. Squabbles over territory, fights over the tranquil waters, arguments over the heath collected. Yet still the population grew, the younger folk were sent out to fend for themselves and travel further into the haunted gullies and higher peaks and given only the older stock to establish their own farms.

Evans

and his wife were one such family to move away from their ancestral home. They migrated with a group of twenty people forming five small families. They took only five milking cows, ten goats, and two dogs. The cattle were stocky creatures, their coats as black as the strange mineral founded under the ground. The goats were sprightly and whimsical, nimble on their feet and humorous in the way they woke the settlers each morning by nibbling at their owners' hair. The group travelled along the base of a great valley for several days then reaching the junction of two huge mountain ranges climbed and climbed and climbed to reach the summit. The milk supply dwindled and the dogs were too tired to hunt for local birds and small animals. The plants bore no berries and the leaves were too bitter to eat. An occasional glint of sunlight against the far away ridge drew the adventurers on and up the great mountain side. They and their stock were tired and hungry and the journey long and dangerous with many slips and tumbles down the slopes undoing hours of clambering. Yet as the first snowflakes drifted down so they reached the summit of the mountain range. Here the vegetation of the alpine zone was sweet and lush; and warm, deep caves were set into the ridge. The families settled. Once the snow season had passed they began to collect the rocks from the ridge to build cottages as their ancestors had when they arrived in Wales. The rock was scarcer here and many boulders were buried into the hillside. The settlers discovered how

 8

to dig these boulders out of the earth's crust and move them to make buildings; large, warm and weatherproof cottages. After a week of mining the earth moved under their feet for the first time. A deep shuddering so deep that a tremor could be seen in the far away ridges too. The matter could not be explained. After some hesitation the settlers continued with their lives. The dogs produced puppies in the early summer, the two cows calved that had been pregnant when they left their ancestral home and the goats bore signs of producing kids in the autumn. Seasons seemed confused since the migration, but life was being reproduced and two human babies would be born in the early spring.

Land tremors and mountain shudders continued into the next winter but the movement had ceased by the peak of the snow season. The pups grew strong and adventurous and look so like their parents, medium length legs, pale yellow red coats with flashes of white markings on their heads and bellies. Their ears were folded forwards and over in deference to their masters: the settlers. As spring approached the pups mimicked their parents in the herding of the stock onto spring pastures and grazing. While the stock were grazing the settlers again began collecting and prying rocks and boulders from the earth's crust. Then the earth began its rumbling again. The tremors became shudders, the shudders massive upheavals and groans, buildings tumbled

and the settlers thought about fleeing back to starvation and the tribal troubles of their ancestral homes.

The decision had been left too late. For as the golden orb of the sun dipped behind the neighbouring snow-capped mountain range the sun turned a brilliant red and gold tinges were seen around the orb. There had been no tremors or shudders for two sunsets but this day the snow-capped mountain heaved upwards and flashes of broad sheets twisting and turning sliced the side of the mountain. The sheets cutting the hillside vertically from ridge to the base of the connecting gully. There was no noise, no noise at all and just the slightest tremble under foot. The settlers stood and watched, the golden orb of the sun was obscured by a serrated skyline as the sheet rose straight up and above the ridge. Two enormous boulders twitched and moved. Then a promontory jerked and turned to face then. The boulders were ears, the vertical sheet met another from the other side of the range and flapped as wings on a bird. The promontory parted as in a mouth and the red fire of the sun could be seen to shoot from the throat. The eye holes were burned through by this powerful red fire and the orbs glowed as with the whole power of the sun but with the seeing ability of eyes. Then the greatest noise ever began and only became louder, and louder. So loud the settlers collapsed from the pain and passed out, as did all their dogs and stock.

When

the settlers came to their senses it was because the dogs and pups were licking their faces and snuffling and whispering into their ears. The village folk now gathered together in the darkness that enveloped their homes and then as a sneaking daylight flitted through they turned to the mountain that had awoken. It was no dream, the mountain range had disappeared. Where the sinister but non-threatening ragged top range had rested, and protected them from the winds of the great land of water, there was nothing; and now the water lapped at the foundations of their own mountain range.

There

was no sign of the mountain or the creature which the whispering of the dogs had named "dragon". As the mountain range had vanished so had the dragon. After a few restless nights the families decided to stay on their own ridge. Occasionally, for the next couple of seasons they could hear a very far off rumble and there was the slightest tremble in the earth at evening. Yet the days were idyllic in the growing season and gentle in the snow season. Then one morning an unknown woman staggered up the steep sides of their mountain range. She told tales of pestilence, death, and destruction. She spoke of vast fires and winds from the land of their Welsh ancestors. The surviving lady, who called herself Cardigaan, was heavy with child and the story sprang from her lips during a difficult birth. She bemoaned the death

of her parents, their parents, her husband and her first born, she foretold a day of great reckoning, fear but then safety. Only she seemed to have survived and the tale was beyond belief. She suckled her newborn child and slowly recovered although she spoke no more. No words passed her lips again in the hearing of the settlers but she recuperated slowly and was particularly fond of the dogs, now numbering twelve for a second litter had been successfully raised.

Another three season cycles passed. The weather become progressively worse and unkind. The snow lingered, the local water stayed frozen for longer, the summer days were chill and windy. The earth began to rumble gently underfoot as of yore and vegetation had trouble thriving and growing. Councils were conducted to discuss possible evacuation and a ballot amongst the families was to be sought on the morrow. The dawn arrived clear, bright and warm. The sun shone and the rocks and buildings warmed. The decision to leave was made conditional on the coldness staying. Day after day, the warmth came back into the area. Yet just as plants began to grow then the heat became too intense and the plants wilted and the leaves burned. The nights were extremely hot and the air dry too. The weak laid down and woke no more, there were several deaths in those

weeks. Evans, now old, woke one morning to see the mountain range as it used to be, lying between his land and the great lake of water. It was very hot and the remaining half dozen dogs lolled around in the cool of the building catching the wispy zephyr off the ocean. But there was no ocean to see, the mountain range had returned and it stifled the zephyr from the great lake of water. Few people and few of the livestock awoke from their heat induced slumbers. Heat was constantly increasing slowly and more died. On the evening of two burials the returned mountain range stirred and began to approach the ruined settlers area. The movement was silent, in fact all was silent again. The movement was slow but definite and the heat began to increase even more. Small rumbles in the heart of the settlers' mountain range seemed to stir the dogs, four remained and all four jumped to their feet, barking in an unusual dry voice. "Dragon, dragon" they snapped. But Evans and the few humans remaining were unmoved, the heat paralyzed them. It was a truly strange sight for as the mountain range slid towards theirs it shrank in size rather than grew. For a moment it seemed to vanish entirely, then there was a rush of steam and hail from the valley that had separated the settlers' mountain from the vanished mountain, and the silence perished. A small red scaly flying creature appeared from the crevice with a gentle but fierce flapping of its wings. The air smelt of rotten eggs and the steam melted the hail to reveal pebbles and rocks catapulted from the valley floor upwards as shooting stars would fall from the heavens but in reverse.

There seemed no escape. Evans, Pembroklyn who was the daughter of Cardigaan, and a couple of the villagers, who alone survived the heat of the summer, now stood and waited for fate to take their lives too.

Pembroklyn

dropped to her knees and called the snapping and snarling dogs to the group of people. The choked and dusty voices of the dogs seemed to still gasp out the words, "Dragon, dragon". She murmured to each dog individually. As with herding the livestock each of the four sank down on their legs and slipped off to work and surround and force the dragon into one of the caves. The old dog who had travelled from the ancestral land with the people, took the left flank and eyed off the dragon until he caught the monster's attention, then as the dragon advanced stealthily forwards on his short legs the old dog rose to his full height and invited the dragon forwards and towards the deep cave. The grandson of the old dog crept on to the far side and followed the dragon forwards. As the dragon skipped forward towards the old dog, the grandson snapped and distracted the dragon's designs on the old dog. The two bitches stalked behind until the old dog had drawn the dragon into the dark cave, but the darkness seemed to scare the dragon for he hesitated. A soft whisper from Pembroklyn reached the dogs as the dragon turned and unfolded its

wings and spat a sheet of flame from its mouth. The old dog and his grandson sent up a volley of cries and yelps and dashed into the cave, scampering up the terraced walls so attracting and drawing the dragon into the cave. As the dragon drew in its wings and breathed out more flame to light the depths of the cavern, the two bitches rushed forward and snapped at the heels of the dragon. Each bitch made contact and the dragon leapt forward crashing its head into the wall.

The dragon stood stunned for a moment then slowly shook its head from side to side, knocking the sides of cavern. It appeared disorientated and flung its head from wall to wall of the cave and a shattering feeling came through the mountain range. All four dogs scampered further up the terraced walls and reached a wide platform, there they sat comfortably and yodelled across the cave and the dragon's head to each other, two being each side of the cave. First a soft whingeing, then the melodious notes of a soul searching song could be heard to pass from one side of the cave to the other. The volume increased, and the melodious Welsh dogs formed a choir not to be matched again for such long periods. The singing lulled the fiery agony of the dragon who swooned and slipped into a heavy sleep. It was heard to rumble and snort as though snoring, as the sun slid out of sight but the dogs continued their singing,

high pitched and clear until the roof of the cave slid down almost silently and sealed the cave entrance.

The people stirred and Pembroklyn walked forwards and handled the rocks that sealed the dogs and dragon into a tomb. She turned and walked back towards the people and shepherded them away from the sealed cave from whence the snoring of the dragon could still be felt in the ground they tread and the softest singing and yodelling of the dogs could be caught occasionally on the wind.

The people became more active and light came back into their eyes as the heat eased over the next few days. The rocks over the cave slid down more compactly and the singing of the dogs was heard no more. Their faithfulness was much talked of and their company sorely missed them for all four seemed to have perished. Their legacy was a return to pleasant seasons for the people and their goats and cattle which now spread far and wide without the dogs to keep them close to the human settlement. As the seasons rolled on, the area again grew abundant vegetation, the only legacy of the dragon, so named by those faithful and missed dogs, was the evolution of an ever growing new mountain promontory. Pembroklyn, as she died, told the settlers not to fear this growth, it was just the mountain absorbing the dragon and its fury.

 23

Many centuries and generations passed and Pembroklyn's daughter produced her own daughters and so these also had children, just as Evans' descendants lived healthy lives and had children too. But amongst all good people there is born a wayward child bent on disrespect and even destruction. Some people talk of a devil placing changeling children in families, others of the perils of inbreeding. In any case the product of generations of this settler colony was not truly evil or bad, just inquisitive and occasionally willful. The mountain promontory had grown as tall as the mountain range itself in the many years and the children had always been told to keep away from the tomb of the dragon and the faithful four. The story of his forebears fascinated the toddler Teifi who was always found crawling or wandering in the area of the cave's sealed entrance. Caught unawares his parents would hear him chanting "doggy, doggy, gee, gee, corgi, corgi". After many instances, they left their rescue of Teifi a shade too late this day.

They arrived as Teifi began to climb up the tumbled rock face and the stones and rocks began to slide and cascade. Teifi was soon buried in the rubble despite trying to run away from the area. The cascading rubble continued to rock and pile up over him and then the villagers involved in the attempted rescue could hear the snoring of the dragon. The insulation of the sealed entrance

being removed the snoring seemed to add to the avalanche effect. Piles and piles of rubble and rock slid from the mountain side and built up around the old village site, Teifi was buried.

A sharp yelp-like sheering of the whole promontory was heard and then a great earthquake could be seen to be rocking the area across the mountain ranges and through to the most distant mountain ranges too. The earth shuddered, the people thought they heard Teifi chanting from the depths of their own range, chanting "Corgi, corgi". Then there was a massive heaving of the earth beneath their feet and a shuddering so powerful that they were rocked from side to side and spun around. One after the other they collapsed where they fell. Water gushed from the now open dragon's tomb. The stream was powerful and rushed as though from a cut artery. The water pelted out of the open tomb and as it did so the small pile of rubble remaining at the entrance caused it to eddy and spin around and as the level increased only then did the water escape and hurtle over the edge and into the valley and so into the ocean. Although unable to stand the settlers could hear the roar of the water and saw it as a river topple over the cliff. There was a ripping, tearing, roaring splintering noise as the mountain, their own mountain range tore slowly downwards. Splitting from top to base just as the other mountain range had been torn from base to summit when the dragon first appeared.

The settlement and its residents were now divided into two by a roaring river and the colony was split further and further apart over the next few days although the earth tremors eased and the settlers could safely collect a little food. The dragon had not reappeared, but steam was seen escaping in blowholes in neighbouring ranges. There was no sign of Teifi. The settlers set up two new villages, divided by the new river. The water course seemed to have no start other than from the dragon's tomb and it was named Teifi.

While no dragon appeared in its original form each village saw for the first time a short legged fur covered creature with upright ears and sparkling eyes. To one side of the river Teifi the pair were black or a light black, perhaps blue in colour, they carried tails and had only short legs. They worked the stock as the dogs of old were said to have driven the dragon into the mountain. Eventually the people of this side of the river accepted the dog-dragon creatures, for the animal was built as the dragon was, yet these creatures sang with the voices of dogs and worked the stock as the dogs of yore had been said to. On the other side of the Teifi the creatures took a different form, they were more alert and active, although they had the upright ear it was smaller and they had no tails. But these fiery red creatures, the same

colour as the ancients spoke of the breath of the dragon needed to be more nimble for the terrain was sharper and more demanding for the herding of the cattle. And this red pair brought many cattle back to the village before asking for shelter and love themselves.

Once a bridge over the Teifi was completed the settlers on each side discussed these wondrous new and helpful creatures and compared them with the descriptions of the famous dogs of the past, and the dragon. One wise old man voiced their thoughts when he spoke of the great mountain range of Rrac splitting to release the dragon, how the local dogs had herded this dragon into the cave and there they had guarded their charge for many generations. When the river Teifi was formed the dogs sacrificed themselves to the dragon and as the river itself destroyed the dragon so four creatures were hewn from the dragon, the four corgis of Teifi's cries had been born and released from the womb of the mountain, the tomb of the dragon.

The four Corgis formed two families and both families were named in honour of the stray woman Cardigann and her daughter Pembroklyn. Of the two dog tribes, the Pembroke took the red of the dragon's skin and breath but lost his tail to the whim of

the dragon. While the Cardigan took the dragon's wings for his ears and his tail for salutation but his glorious coat was singed to wondrous shades of black and tan or blue by the dragon's fiery breath. Each of the families shared the dragon's sparkling eye, long muzzle, upright ears, long low body, and short legs. Not unnaturally, over the generations, members of each dog family have united but essentially there are still two distinct products of the Welsh dragon for if the two families were to merge as a single the dragon would be reborn. The beasts of the Corgi's chosen vocation, now the dragon had been tamed, were the wily cattle that thrived on steep and rough mountain sides, there was no longer any need for wings or fire breath - well not often.

This has been the story of the Corgis of Wales as faithfully handed down through time by the second daughter of a second daughter.

As I said the last of this twenty two generations has now left earth but in her passing because of the confusion amongst Corgi guardians she has bid me tell you, and all, the tale of the Welsh dragon, the child Teifi and his naming of the Corgi, and the formation of the Cardigan and Pembroke breeds. These are dogs of the mountain, dogs that can outwit wily hill cattle, dogs that know their master's business. Dogs that are sure footed, healthy and the size of the dragon of Wales as it was in true life.

Made in the USA
Monee, IL
08 May 2022